PRESENTED TO: Missy Turbyfill

Recognizing interest in family involvement
and the importance of reading.

2000 minutes

ECIA CHAPTER I
SCHOOL CITY OF HAMMOND

Jo-Jo
The Melon Donkey

MICHAEL MORPURGO

ILLUSTRATED BY CHRIS MOLAN

Prentice-Hall Books for Young Readers
A DIVISION OF SIMON & SCHUSTER, INC.
NEW YORK

*For
Lis and Alex*

Published by Prentice-Hall Books for Young Readers, A Division of Simon &
Schuster, Inc., Simon & Schuster Building, Rockefeller Center, 1230 Avenue
of the Americas, New York, NY 10020. First published in Great Britain by
Belitha Press Ltd.; Prentice-Hall Books for Young Readers is a trademark of
Simon & Schuster, Inc.

Art Director: Treld Bicknell

Printed and bound by South China Printing Co., Hong Kong

10 9 8 7 6 5 4 3 2 1

Library of Congress Cataloging-in-Publication Data

Morpurgo, Michael.
   Jo-Jo the melon donkey.

   Summary: A mistreated donkey in Renaissance Venice gains self-respect
after meeting the Doge's kind daughter and becoming a hero during a
devastating flood.
   1. Donkeys — Juvenile fiction. [1. Donkeys — Fiction. 2. Self-respect —
Fiction. 3. Venice (Italy) — Fiction] I. Molan, Chris, ill. II. Title.
PZ10.3.M714Jo   1987   [Fic]   87-6993
ISBN 0-13-510009-7

Jo-Jo was a donkey. His father had been a donkey before him, and his mother as well; and so of course Jo-Jo had to be a donkey whether he liked it or not. And he did not like it, not one bit. No donkey ever does.

Jo-Jo was only a very little donkey when he took his first drink in the stream and saw himself in the water. From that moment he knew he was ugly, and so he always drank with his eyes closed, as all donkeys do. Jo-Jo was only a little older when his master first took a whip to him, and from that moment on he knew he was a slave and lowered his head in shame, as all donkeys do.

Work began early every morning for Jo-Jo. At first light his master would load him with so many melons that he could hardly walk, and then he would be driven out of the village and down the dusty road towards the great city of Venice. If he ever stopped to complain he was beaten. If he ever stopped to rest he was beaten.

Jo-Jo loved Venice. It was his city. He loved the canals and the bridges, the little squares and the sound of the church bells ringing out over the rooftops. He loved to stand and watch the water lapping around the houses, almost as if it wanted to suck the city back into the sea.

All day long his master would haul him down the narrow footpaths of Venice that run alongside the canals, and Jo-Jo would call out, "Melons, melons, melons for sale." His braying would echo down the canals and into the squares, and everyone would know it was Jo-Jo the melon donkey and come running with their money. And all the while the flies came to torment him and would not go away.

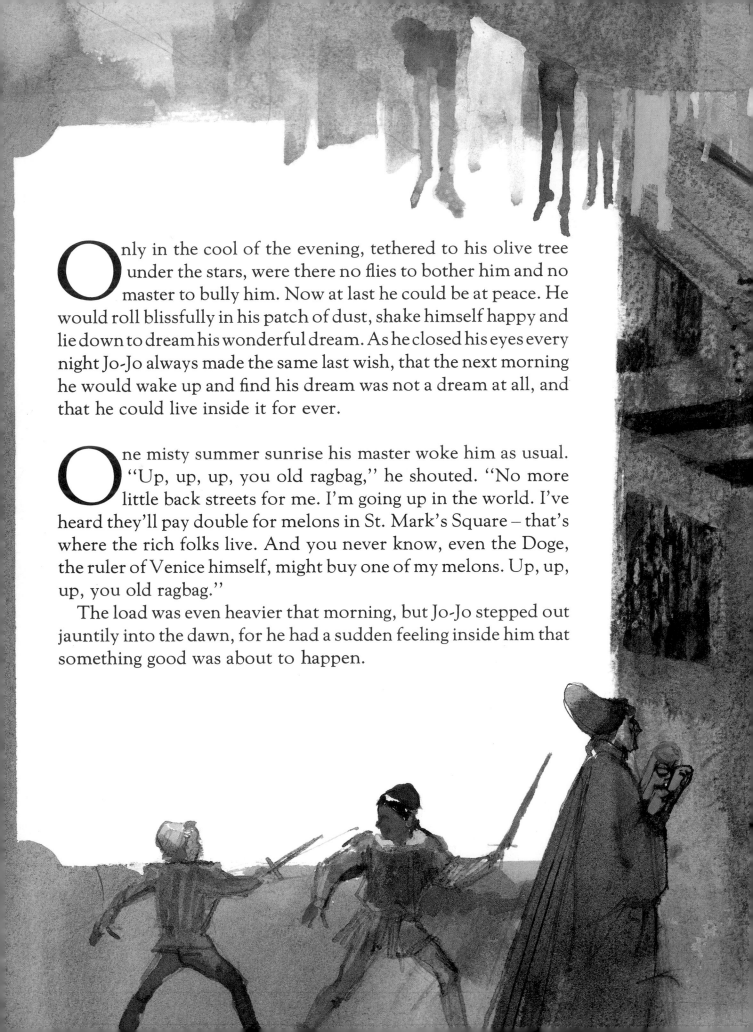

Only in the cool of the evening, tethered to his olive tree under the stars, were there no flies to bother him and no master to bully him. Now at last he could be at peace. He would roll blissfully in his patch of dust, shake himself happy and lie down to dream his wonderful dream. As he closed his eyes every night Jo-Jo always made the same last wish, that the next morning he would wake up and find his dream was not a dream at all, and that he could live inside it for ever.

One misty summer sunrise his master woke him as usual. "Up, up, up, you old ragbag," he shouted. "No more little back streets for me. I'm going up in the world. I've heard they'll pay double for melons in St. Mark's Square – that's where the rich folks live. And you never know, even the Doge, the ruler of Venice himself, might buy one of my melons. Up, up, up, you old ragbag."

The load was even heavier that morning, but Jo-Jo stepped out jauntily into the dawn, for he had a sudden feeling inside him that something good was about to happen.

By the time they reached St. Mark's Square the sun was high in the sky and it was already full of people. "Don't know why I never thought of this before," said his master, unloading the melons. "This is the place for us, right in front of the Cathedral. We'll sell them all in no time. Sing out, you old ragbag you, sing out."

"Melons, melons, melons for sale," Jo-Jo brayed, and his cry rang around the square.

Everyone in St. Mark's Square stopped and turned and looked. And then one of them began to laugh, and to point, and then another and another until the entire square was filled with laughter. "Beauty and the beast!" they cried. "Beauty and the beast!"

"What do you mean? What are you laughing at?" asked Jo-Jo's master. "You've seen a donkey before, haven't you? What's so funny?"

"Above your head," they cried. "Look above your head!" Jo-Jo and his master looked up. Behind and above them, burnished gold and glowing in the sun, stood the four golden horses of Venice, the four most beautiful horses in all the world. Jo-Jo had never seen anything so wonderful. He could not take his eyes off them. "Beauty and the beast!" roared the crowd. "Beauty and the beast!" And his master laughed with them. Jo-Jo hung his head in shame and wished he was dead.

All morning the people came to point and stare, but they bought no melons. "Take your filthy donkey to the back streets," they said, looking down their noses at Jo-Jo. "That's where he belongs. And you can take your melons too. We don't eat melons here. They're not for the likes of us."

Then as noon chimed on the Cathedral clock, the great doors of the Doge's Palace opened and a little girl ran out into St. Mark's Square, a nurse bustling after her. "Come back, come back," she cried. "You know you're not allowed out of the Palace."

"But I want a melon," said the little girl. "And anyway I don't like being cooped up in that Palace all day. I've got no friends to play with and I'm bored."

"It's the Doge's daughter," someone whispered; and soon every-one was there, bowing and curtseying as she passed. She ignored them all and made straight for the pile of melons beside Jo-Jo. "She's going to buy a melon," whispered someone else.

"Never! She wouldn't! The Doge's daughter? Buy a melon? Never!"

"She is, she is!" And indeed she was.

"How much do you want for one of your melons?" she asked Jo-Jo's master.

"Such an honor, Highness. Such an honor," replied Jo-Jo's master, bowing and scraping and wringing his dirty hands. "For you, Highness, it's a gift. I have the best melons in all of Venice, Highness, and this one is for you."

"Thank you," said the Doge's daughter, taking the melon; and then she noticed Jo-Jo standing beside his master.

Jo-Jo was panting in the heat, trying to forget the flies around his eyes. "And is this your donkey?" asked the Doge's daughter.

"Unfortunately, yes, Highness," said Jo-Jo's master. "I call him Jo-Jo, a wretched ragbag of a creature; but I'm a poor man and it's the best a poor man can do. You can't judge a man by his donkey, Highness."

"He has such sad, kind eyes," said the Doge's daughter. "He looks so unhappy." And she reached out and stroked Jo-Jo on his neck. She patted his shoulder and smoothed his nose. Jo-Jo had never been patted in all his life, and his knees weakened with joy.

"Really, Your Highness," said the nurse, taking the Doge's daughter's arm and leading her away. "Now I'm going to have to wash you all over again. Fancy touching that filthy creature. Can't you see there's flies all over him? Now come along back to the Palace before your father sees you." And she hustled the little girl away and back into the Palace.

Jo-Jo closed his eyes and held the picture of the little girl in his mind so that it would never go away.

Within a few minutes all the melons were sold. Suddenly anyone who was anyone in St. Mark's Square was eating melons. After all, what was good enough for the Doge's daughter was good enough for them.

So every day that summer Jo-Jo came to St. Mark's Square loaded with melons, and stood under the four golden horses in front of the Cathedral. And every day the Doge's daughter came at noon for her melon. And every time she came she never failed to smile at Jo-Jo. She would always talk gently to him and smooth his nose before she left. These were the moments of the day that Jo-Jo longed for and treasured.

One afternoon, while his master dozed under his hat and the whole city slumbered through the heat of the day, Jo-Jo was gazing up at the four shining golden horses, as he often did. They were everything a donkey longed to be but never could be. Suddenly, as he looked at them all the sadness of his life welled up inside him and he cried out: "Oh, why can't I be like you? Oh, why can't I be like you?" At that his master woke from his snoring sleep and beat him.

"How dare you wake me like that?" he roared. "No use talking to those horses, you stupid old ragbag you. They can't hear. Can't you see they're nothing but statues? Statues can't hear. Statues can't speak."

But Jo-Jo knew they could.

The very next morning, just after Jo-Jo and his master arrived in the Square, the Doge's Herald came out of the Palace, surrounded by soldiers. Trumpets sounded and a crowd gathered to listen.

"Be it known to one and all," the Herald proclaimed, "that the Doge intends to purchase the finest horse in the city for his daughter's birthday. A price of ten thousand ducats will be paid. The horse will be chosen at noon this very day, for today is the Doge's daughter's birthday. Let the bells ring out!" And the bells of the great Cathedral began to peal, sending the pigeons soaring out over the lagoon and away.

Jo-Jo stood and watched the horses arriving in the Square all that morning. Every one of them was finer than the one before and every one of them made him feel smaller and uglier than ever. They were brushed and buffed until they shone, plaited and pulled until not a hair was out of place. There were black Arabian stallions with tossing heads, snorting as they came. There were gray Spanish mares with flowing manes, prancing as they came. Soon all the finest horses in the city were assembled and a huge crowd thronged the Square.

As the noon bell sounded the great Doge himself came out of the Palace, his daughter beside him; and the grand parade began. The crowd clapped and cheered as the horses trotted by until there were no more to come.

The Doge did not have to call for silence. All of Venice was waiting to hear his choice. "My daughter is ten years old today," he said, "and at ten she is quite old enough to be able to choose for herself." He turned to his daughter. "Now my child," he said, "you may choose whichever one of them pleases you most. It is your birthday."

The Doge's daughter walked slowly along the line of waiting horses, and then at last she turned away and pointed. "Over there!" she said, pointing towards the four golden horses.

"But my child," said the Doge, "you cannot have the golden horses. They belong to the people of Venice. They've been there for hundreds of years."

"Not them," the Doge's daughter said. "I want that one, the one that's standing by the melons, Father."

The crowd gasped. "But that's a donkey! You want a donkey?" the Doge cried.

"Yes, Father," said the Doge's daughter. And Jo-Jo was even happier at that moment than when he was rolling in his dust patch under his olive tree. He was not ugly after all! He could not be! The Doge's daughter had chosen *him*, a donkey, from amongst the finest horses in the city of Venice!

"I forbid it," said the Doge, "I absolutely forbid it. I cannot have a daughter of mine, a daughter of the Doge of Venice, riding around on some flea-bitten donkey!"

"But I don't want to ride around on him," said the Doge's daughter. "I want him to be my friend. I have no friends to play with, Father. And you did say I could choose any one I wanted. You said I could, Father. And he's not flea-bitten at all. He's beautiful. He's much more beautiful than any of the others."

"Don't argue with me," thundered the Doge. "You could have picked the finest horse in the land and you chose that walking carpet. Look at him, how he stands there hanging his great shaggy head. And his ears, look at his ears! And his feet are curled up like Turkish slippers. Why, he's a blot on creation!"

"Father," said the Doge's daughter, her eyes filling with tears, "if I cannot have Jo-Jo as my present, then I don't want anything."

"Very well," said the Doge. "You shall have your wish. You will go without a present. Go back into the Palace and go to your room at once."

But the Doge's daughter ran across the Square to where Jo-Jo stood and put her arms around his neck. "Come to the Palace tonight," she whispered, "and wait outside my window. I shall climb down and we shall run away together. Be there, Jo-Jo. Do not fail me."

Whatever names they called Jo-Jo as his master dragged him away through the crowds, he did not mind. When they threw their empty melon skins at him, he did not mind. For the first time in his life Jo-Jo was proud he was a donkey. At last he could hold his head up high, and he did.

Back in the village even his master bragged how it was his donkey that had shamed all the fine noblemen and their fancy horses; but once on his own with Jo-Jo he was as nasty as ever. "Don't go getting any grand ideas inside that ugly head of yours, you old ragbag," he said. "You're just a donkey, and a pretty poor one at that, and don't you forget it. Once a donkey, always a donkey. And what's more you'll have no supper tonight after what you've cost me. Do you realize, if you hadn't been a donkey I'd have been richer by ten thousand ducats tonight, ten thousand ducats, d'you hear me?"

Jo-Jo heard him, but he was not listening. He was making plans.

Jo-Jo did not sleep that night. He was too excited. He waited until all was quiet and then set to work. In the black of the night Jo-Jo bit through the rope that tethered him to his olive tree and made his way carefully through the sleeping village, down the road and back into the city of Venice. It was a wild, wet and windy night. No one heard Jo-Jo hurrying through the empty streets, trotting over the little bridges, across St. Mark's Square towards the Doge's Palace.

And then he heard the voices. At first he thought it must have been the wind whistling through the towers and spires of the city. But then he looked up. The four golden horses spoke as one, their voices a whisper on the wind, but quite clear. "Little donkey, little donkey," they said. "Listen to us, little donkey. The sea is coming in. The sea is coming in. Only you can save the people. You must wake them and warn them. Tell them to leave, little donkey. Do it quickly or it will be too late. They will all drown if you do not save them. Hurry, little donkey, hurry!"

Jo-Jo galloped across the Square until he reached the water's edge and looked out over the lagoon. Sure enough, he could hear the waves rolling in towards him from the sea. He felt the water washing over his hooves and saw it running down over the stones and into the Square behind him. He lifted his head, took the deepest breath of his life, and then he brayed and he brayed and he brayed until his head ached with it.

In her bedroom in the Palace the Doge's daughter was waiting for Jo-Jo. When she heard him calling, she let herself down out of her window and ran over to him. "Not so loud, Jo-Jo," she said. "You'll wake everyone up." And then she too heard the distant roar of the sea and heard the waves rolling in. She felt the water round her ankles and understood why Jo-Jo was braying. She knew at once what had to be done.

With the Doge's daughter on his back, Jo-Jo rode braying through the city streets waking everyone up. "What?" they shouted, opening their windows and looking out into the dark streets. "What, melons at this time of night?"

"No, no!" cried the Doge's daughter. "The sea has broken in and the city is flooding. Save yourselves! Save yourselves!" And all the while the sea came in, flooding the Square and the Cathedral and the Doge's Palace itself. Woken by Jo-Jo's braying, the people of Venice ran for their lives.

The Doge sent out his soldiers into every corner of the city, into every house so that no one would be left behind; and Jo-Jo, the melon donkey, with the Doge's daughter on his back, guided the children and the old people to safety down the flooding streets. And all the time the waters rose and rose around them. Houses crumbled and the great bell tower in the Square came crashing down into the water.

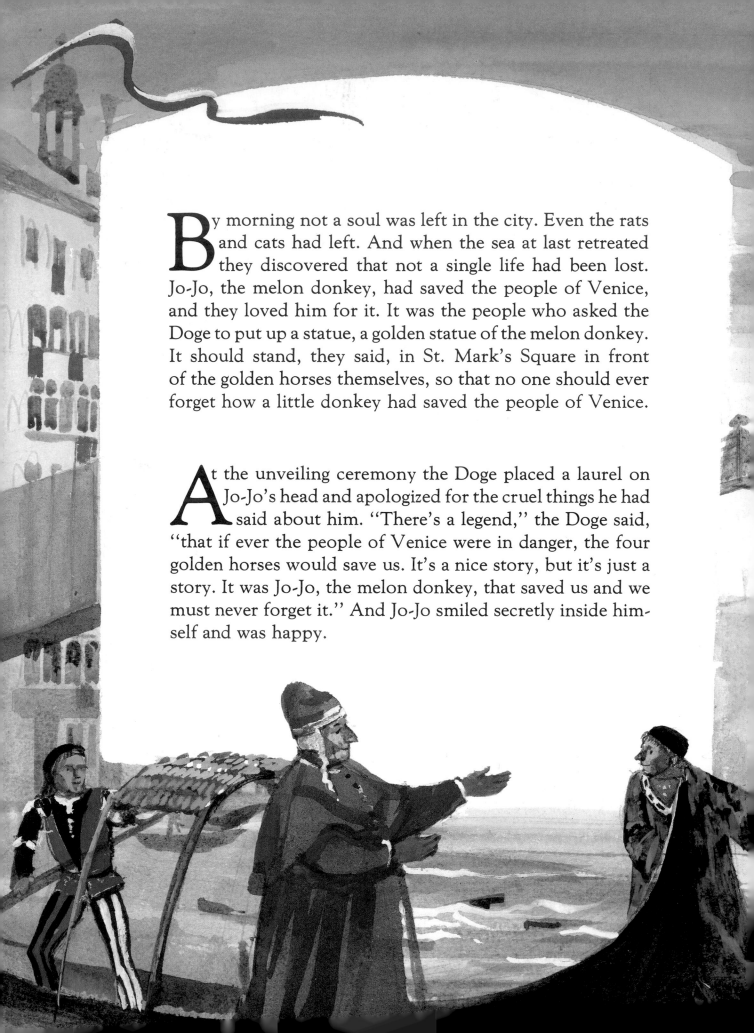

By morning not a soul was left in the city. Even the rats and cats had left. And when the sea at last retreated they discovered that not a single life had been lost. Jo-Jo, the melon donkey, had saved the people of Venice, and they loved him for it. It was the people who asked the Doge to put up a statue, a golden statue of the melon donkey. It should stand, they said, in St. Mark's Square in front of the golden horses themselves, so that no one should ever forget how a little donkey had saved the people of Venice.

At the unveiling ceremony the Doge placed a laurel on Jo-Jo's head and apologized for the cruel things he had said about him. "There's a legend," the Doge said, "that if ever the people of Venice were in danger, the four golden horses would save us. It's a nice story, but it's just a story. It was Jo-Jo, the melon donkey, that saved us and we must never forget it." And Jo-Jo smiled secretly inside himself and was happy.

So Jo-Jo was never again made to carry anything; except, that is, for the garlands of flowers that the people put around his neck every day when he went out of the Doge's Palace for his walk. For he became the Doge's daughter's donkey (and you must not say that too fast), and was her constant companion for the rest of his life – and donkeys do live for donkey's years, you know.